ABDO Publishing Company is the exclusive school and library distributor of Rabbit Ears Books.

Library bound edition 2005.

Copyright © 1995 Rabbit Ears Entertainment, LLC.,
S. Norwalk, Connecticut.

Library of Congress Cataloging-in-Publication Data

Metaxas, Eric.
 The emperor's new clothes / retold by Eric Metaxas ; illustrated by Robert Van Nutt.
  p. cm.
 "Rabbit Ears books."
 Summary: Two rascally weavers convince the emperor they are making him beautiful new clothes, visible only to those fit for their posts, but during a royal procession in which he first wears them, a child whispers that the emperor has nothing on.
 ISBN 1-59197-746-0
 [1. Fairy tales.] I. Van Nutt, Robert, ill. II. Andersen, H. C. (Hans Christian), 1805-1875. Kejserens nye klaeder. III. Title.

PZ8.M55Em 2005
[E]—dc22

2004046696

All Rabbit Ears books are reinforced library binding
and manufactured in the United States of America.

ABDO
Publishing Company

Written by Hans Christian Andersen

The Emperor's New Clothes

Retold by Eric Metaxas

Illustrated by Robert Van Nutt

Rabbit Ears Books

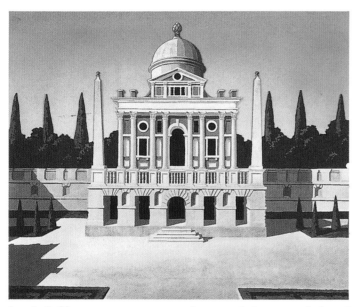

Many, many years ago, there lived an Emperor. He was so hopelessly in love with beautiful new clothes that he spent all of his money on them. He took no interest whatever in the theater. He did not trouble himself in the least about his soldiers; nor did he care to go either hunting or riding in the park…unless, of course, it gave him the opportunity to show off his new clothes. He had different garments for each hour of the day, and just as in most countries one might safely assume that the king would be in his throne room, or in his council chamber, it was always said of this monarch, "The Emperor is in his dressing room."

Life was jolly in the large town where the Emperor held court, and each day hosts of new visitors would arrive. One day two rogues, calling themselves weavers, requested an audience with the Emperor. They claimed to be able to weave the most beautiful cloth imaginable.

They said that not only were the colors and patterns of their cloth exceptionally beautiful, but any clothing made from this material possessed the curious quality of being completely invisible to anyone who was either undeserving of his position or impossibly dull-witted. "Those must, indeed, be splendid clothes!" thought the Emperor. "If I had clothes made from that material, I'd be able to tell at once which men in my empire were unfit for their posts. I would even be able to distinguish the wise men from the fools. Oh yes, I must certainly order some of that material to be woven for me at once!" And the Emperor gave the two weavers a great deal of money in advance, so that they could begin their work immediately.

They set up two looms and began busily weaving away, but in truth, there was nothing whatsoever on their shuttles. They asked for the finest silk and the purest gold and silver thread, but hid every last bit of it away in their own bags while they pretended to be working late into the night on the imperial cloth.

Before long, everyone in the town had heard of the wonderful quality that the cloth was said to possess, and each person was quite anxious to discover how unfit for his job or how incredibly dim-witted his neighbor was. The Emperor was anxious as well. "I should like to know how those weavers are progressing with my cloth," he thought, but immediately became uneasy when he remembered that anyone who was dull-witted or unfit for his office would be unable to see it. "To be sure," he thought, "I have no need to be concerned for my own Imperial Self…" Nevertheless, he decided to send someone else first… just to see how things were progressing, you understand. "I shall send my faithful old Minister to the weavers," thought the Emperor. "He will be best able to judge the material, for he is a wise man and no one is better fit for his office."

So the trusted old Minister stepped into the room where the weavers were busily working, but when he turned his gaze to the looms, a very troubled expression came over his face. "Heaven preserve me!" thought the old Minister, opening his eyes as wide as possible. The weavers bade the distressed official to step a bit closer and asked if he did not admire the exquisite pattern and beautiful coloring.

They pointed to the empty looms and the poor old Minister opened his eyes even wider. He looked and looked but he could see nothing, for of course there was nothing to see.

"Well, My Lord Minister," said one of the scoundrels, "have you nothing to say about the cloth?"

"Oh yes, it is very beautiful, most admirable indeed!" proclaimed the old Minister. "Such a pattern! And the colors... it's remarkable! I shall certainly tell the Emperor that I am well pleased by it!"

"Thank you, My Lord Minister, we are very pleased to hear it!" said the weavers, for indeed, they were. They then proceeded to describe wonderful colors and exquisite patterns to him in full detail. They even went so far as to point to what they said was a complicated fish motif in the border. The old Minister listened very carefully to everything the weavers had to say so that he would be able to describe the cloth to the Emperor. The knaves then asked for more gold and silver thread, saying that it was necessary in order to complete what they had begun. What they really did was to hide all that was given to them in their own bags and continue working away with as much activity as before at the empty looms.

Soon afterwards the Emperor sent another of his trusted officials to see how the work was progressing, and to ask whether it would soon be finished. The same thing happened to this gentleman as to the old Minister. He looked at the looms from all sides, but could see nothing at all but the empty frames.

"Is it not a fine piece of work? Does it not appear as beautiful to Your Excellency as it did to My Lord, the Minister?" asked one of the weavers. The frightened official did his best to recall the old Minister's description of the cloth. He feigned delight in the beautiful colors and the originality of the patterns. He even went so far as to express his particular admiration for the fish border motif.

"Begging Your Excellency's pardon, but these are birds, the fish motif is over here," said one of the weavers, pointing to another part of the loom.

"Oh, of course, of course," said the confused courtier. "The utter magnificence of the cloth quite dazzled me."

"Your words of praise please us no end, Your Excellency!" proclaimed the rogues, bowing and smiling all the while.

"Your Imperial Majesty, it is absolutely enchanting!" exclaimed the official when he returned to the Emperor. "Really, one must see it for oneself! Words can hardly capture it!" And very soon, everyone in the imperial city was discussing the Emperor's wonderful cloth as though they had seen it with their own eyes.

Finally, the Emperor decided that he would like to see his costly cloth for himself while it was still on the loom. And so, with a large company of courtiers, among whom were the two trusted officials who had already praised the imaginary cloth, he went to inspect the work of the two clever weavers. When they heard the royal party approaching, the two rogues pretended to work harder than ever at the empty looms.

"Is it not magnificent?" proclaimed the two trusted officials. "If Your Majesty would only be so kind as to gaze upon it! Observe, what a splendid design! What glorious colors!" And at the same time they pointed to the empty looms; for they imagined that everyone but themselves could see this magnificent piece of workmanship.

The Emperor's face turned four distinct colors behind his frozen smile. "Ah, yes," he proclaimed aloud to everyone in the room; "it is beautiful. It is ah… very, very beautiful. It has our highest approval." As he said this he nodded his head approvingly while staring at the empty looms, for on no count would he admit that he could not see what two of the officers of his court had praised so highly. The entire company that had come along stared at the looms as well, and was rather quiet, but as soon as the Emperor had spoken, they too exclaimed over the excellent quality of the nonexistent cloth.

"Oh, yes, yes, it is beautiful. It is very, very beautiful!" they all exclaimed. They then advised the Emperor to commission a suit of clothes to be made of this splendid material so that he might wear it in the great Festival Parade that would soon take place.

"We are terribly pleased to see that his Majesty finds favor with our humble efforts," said one of the weavers. "We think it is rather special ourselves, if we may be so bold as to say so."

The Emperor nodded his agreement heartily. "It is outstanding! It is stupendous! It is very, very stupendous!" exclaimed the courtiers, for everyone was equally delighted.

The Emperor then awarded the two rascals an Imperial Decoration to wear and bestowed upon them the title of "Gentlemen Weavers of the Imperial Loom."

"But you are too kind, Your Majesty!" they said, shedding tears of joy, "Oh, but Your Majesty is much, much too kind!"

The two swindlers sat up the entire night before the Grand Festival Parade was to take place. They used no less than sixteen candles to illuminate the room in which they were working so that everyone would notice how eager they were to complete the Emperor's new clothes. They pretended to remove the material from the looms. They snipped elaborate patterns in the air with their scissors, and they stitched away using needles without any thread. "See!" they finally announced, "the Emperor's new clothes are ready!"

And now the Emperor with his noblest courtiers came to receive the finished garments. The two rogues raised their hands in the air as though they were holding something for him to see.

"Here are Your Imperial Majesty's britches!" they announced. "Here is the doublet! Here is the mantle! The whole suit is as light as a spider's web; one might fancy one were wearing nothing at all, but that is precisely the beauty of it!"

"How true," chimed the courtiers, "how very, very true!"

"If Your Imperial Majesty would be so kind as to remove your clothes, we will dress you in the new suit here in front of the looking-glass," said the weavers. The Emperor removed all his clothes and the weavers pretended to dress him in one piece after another of the fabulous new garments. Finally, they pretended to fasten his long trailing mantle about his shoulders.

Then one of the weavers put his hand to his mouth and looked quite troubled. He whispered something into the ear of the other weaver, and soon he too looked terribly troubled. "Would Your Majesty be so kind as to stand quite still?" one of them asked very gravely. "It seems that we've neglected to trim off a certain thread."

They began circling around the Emperor very carefully, as though they were sneaking up on a rabbit. Then one of them suddenly lunged in and much to the consternation of the Emperor, snipped his scissors with a great flourish. "Got it!" he exclaimed loudly. "Oh, now Your Majesty does look magnificent! Yes, yes. Very, very magnificent! Oh, oh, oh, someone hold me, for I think I shall faint from sheer ecstasy!"

The Emperor stood in front of the mirror, staring at his naked reflection.

"Oh, how wonderful His Majesty looks!" the courtiers cried. "How perfectly everything fits! Such a pattern! Magnificent colors! Truly Imperial! These are indeed Royal Robes!"

"The ceremonial canopy which is to be borne over Your Majesty in today's procession is waiting outside," announced the Chief Master of the Ceremonies most ceremoniously.

"Well, I am quite ready," said the Emperor. "Do my new clothes not suit me handsomely?" Then he turned once more to the mirror, pretending to admire his magnificent garments. The Imperial Ministers who were to carry the long train of the Emperor's cloak both stooped over and appeared to lift something up from the floor.

They walked along behind the Emperor, holding their hands in the air stiffly, as though they were actually carrying the train of the Royal Mantle.

When the Emperor appeared in the procession, under the ceremonial canopy, everyone in the streets and all those watching from their windows exclaimed:

"Oh! the Emperor's new clothes are the most beautiful garments ever seen! What an exquisite train there is to the cloak! How graceful the fit! Such colors, aaah!" In short, no one would admit that he could not see these much admired clothes, because, in doing so, he would have declared himself either a simpleton or unfit for his office. Never before had the Emperor's clothes met with such unanimous approval.

Suddenly from the crowd a small child cried out: "But the Emperor has no clothes on!"

"Hear what the innocent one says!" exclaimed the child's father; and what the child had said was whispered from one to another through the crowd: "He has nothing on! The Emperor has no clothes on!"

"But he has nothing on at all!" cried all the people at last. And the Emperor cringed, for he knew that what they said was absolutely true.

"The procession must continue all the same," he thought to himself, and he looked straight ahead and held himself more stiffly and more imperially than ever before, and the chamberlains followed closely behind, holding on to the imaginary train.